USBORNE BIBLE TALES
The Good Samaritan

Retold by Heather Amery

Designed by Maria Wheatley

Illustrated by Norman Young

Language consultant: Betty Root
Series editor: Jenny Tyler

This is Jesus.

A man said to him, "God says we must be kind to people. But which people?" Jesus told him this story.

There was a man who was a Jew.

He lived in Jerusalem. One day he started on a long journey to Jericho. He had to walk all the way.

He was alone.

He knew it was dangerous to go on his own. People usually went with other people because of robbers.

Suddenly he saw some robbers.

They ran up to him, shouting and waving sticks.
The man was frightened and tried to run away.

The robbers caught the man.

They beat him with their sticks. They knocked him down and kicked him while he lay on the ground.

They stole everything.

The robbers took most of the man's clothes. They stole his money and his bag. Then they ran away.

The man was badly wounded.

He lay bleeding on the dusty ground. He was so badly hurt, he could not get up or call for help.

Soon a priest came by.

He looked at the wounded man, but he didn't stop.
He made his donkey hurry away down the road.

Then another man came along.

He worked in the temple in Jerusalem. He saw the man but he didn't stop. He hurried down the road.

Then a third man came along.

He was a Samaritan. Although the Samaritans and the Jews hated each other, this man stopped.

The Samaritan got off his donkey.

He poured oil on the man's wounds to soothe them and wine to heal them. Then he bandaged them.

He helped the man to stand up.

The Samaritan lifted the man onto his donkey. Then he led the donkey down the road to the city of Jericho.

They stopped at an inn.

The Samaritan put the man to bed for the night and made him comfortable. He bought him supper.

The Samaritan left the next morning.

He paid the innkeeper. "Look after this man," he said.
"I'll pay any extra bills when I come this way again."

"Which man was kind?" asked Jesus.

"The Samaritan," said the man. "Yes," said Jesus,
"We should be kind to anyone who needs our help."